For Hailey

~HW

For U...

STRIPES PUBLISHING
An imprint of Little Tiger Press
1 The Coda Centre, 189 Munster Road,
London SW6 6AW

A paperback original
First published in Great Britain in 2014

ISBN: 978-1-84715-465-1

Holly Webb Illustrated by Marion Lindsay

Maisie Hitchins

The Case of the Spilled Ink

STRIPES

31 Albion Street, London

Attic:
Maisie's grandmother and Sally the maid

Third floor:
Miss Lane's rooms

Second floor:
Room to let

First floor:
Professor Tobin's rooms

Ground floor:
Entrance hall, sitting room and dining room

Basement:
Maisie's room, kitchen and yard entrance

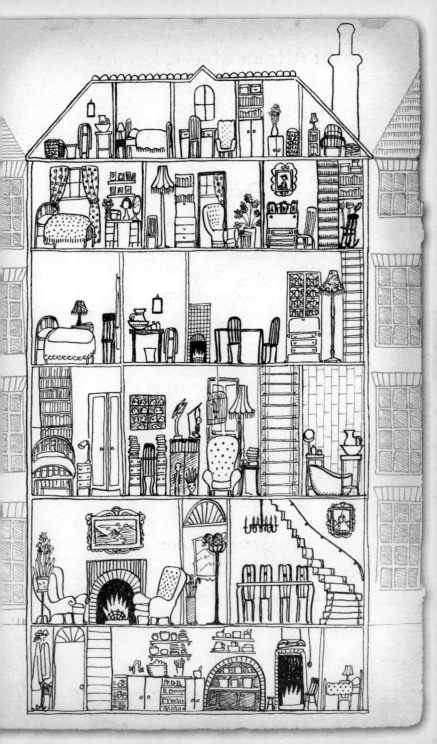

"You're really going to go?" Maisie stared at her friend Alice in surprise. "But won't it be strange? I mean, you've never been to school before. And it's a boarding school! You'll have to live there, with all those other girls!"

Alice didn't answer for a moment. She stroked her white cat, Snowflake, who was stretched out on her lap, and watched

7

Snowflake's kittens chasing each other in and out of the chair legs. "I know," she said at last, very quietly. "I'm to go next week. I'm a bit frightened, Maisie, to be honest. That's why I asked you to come. I wanted to have someone to talk to. I don't really know what it will be like, living with lots of other girls."

Maisie nodded. She didn't think she would like it at all.

"But Papa is so happy, and I do very much like Miss Darling – I mean, oh, I still don't know quite what to call her. I keep thinking of her as my governess, and then remembering that they're married. But I don't mind her being my new mother, I think. I want them to be able to go to Italy on their wedding trip, without having to worry about me. And we haven't any relatives I could stay with, and Papa says I can't stay in the house on my own, not for three whole months. So school it has to be."

"But what happens when they come back?" Maisie asked. "Will you stay at school?"

"Papa says that I can stay there if I like it, or they'll find another governess. Miss Darling said she would be quite happy to go on teaching me, but Papa thought that might be strange." She sighed, and then looked up with a tiny smile. "At least Papa has convinced Miss Prenderby, whose school it is, that I must be allowed to take Snowflake, and Blanche and Lulu. I couldn't bear to leave them behind."

Maisie nodded. She would miss her dog Eddie terribly if she had to go away without him. At the moment he was being looked after down in the kitchens by the cook.

He and Snowflake disliked each other very much, and showed it. Maisie just hoped he was behaving himself. She sighed heavily.

"I'm the one being sent off to boarding school, Maisie!" Alice giggled. "What's the matter?"

Maisie gave a little shudder. "Eddie. I only hope he's behaving. He got us into awful trouble on the way here. We walked past a lady with a little lap dog – you know, a really fluffy one that doesn't walk, just gets carried everywhere. That was the problem, she was carrying it and I thought it was part of the fur on her jacket! If I'd seen there was a dog I'd have put Eddie on his lead. And it was so tiny, I think Eddie thought it was a rat. You know what he's like about rats…"

"Oh dear… Did he chase it?"

"Not really… He didn't have to. It didn't

run away, it was too scared. It just stayed
snuggled up inside the lady's jacket while
Eddie barked and barked, and tried to jump
up at it. He got mud all over her dress."

Maisie shuddered as she remembered.
"We ran away instead," she whispered.
"She actually started to call for a constable.
So I picked up Eddie and just ran!"

Alice clapped her hand across her mouth. "How awful!" she whispered through her fingers, but her eyes were wide and fascinated. "You do have such adventures, Maisie…" She sighed. "I never have adventures. Even that ghost we thought we'd found when we stayed at that eerie house in the country turned out to be darling Snowflake!" She rubbed Snowflake's ears, and the white cat purred graciously. "And there certainly won't be any adventures at Miss Prenderby's Academy. Papa assures me it's a most *proper* establishment."

Maisie wrinkled her nose in disgusted sympathy, and Alice nodded sadly. "All the other girls are very ladylike, apparently. There's even one who's distantly related to the queen. And three Honourables – you know, the daughters of lords. Papa said Miss

Prenderby was extremely keen to tell him that."

Maisie frowned. "They aren't going to be very keen on me visiting then, are they? I don't look grand enough to hobnob with the daughters of lords."

"Don't worry, Maisie," Alice assured her quickly. "I made Papa tell her that you had to be allowed to visit me. That's part of the reason he chose a school in London, after all. I don't think Miss Prenderby was very happy about friends visiting, but Papa is paying her an awful lot of money. She couldn't really say no." She smiled at Maisie and stood up, draping Snowflake over her shoulder like a smart fur stole. "Now you'd better come and see the worst thing about going away. It's a present from Papa. I can't bear to leave it!"

"Can't you take it with you?" Maisie asked.

Alice giggled. "Not really. He had it made for Miss Darling and me, so we can spend time as mother and daughter together. It's in the garden, so we can go out through the kitchens and bring Eddie with us. Snowflake doesn't really like it outside anyway."

It was true – as soon as Alice opened the bedroom door, Snowflake sniffed at the corridor in an unimpressed sort of way, and jumped from Alice's shoulder back to the armchair. Alice giggled again. "See?"

Eddie greeted them delightedly in the kitchen, dancing round Maisie as though he hadn't seen her in months. Maisie inspected him anxiously, but she couldn't see any telltale meaty stains around his chops – perhaps he'd managed not to steal anything. Although the cook still seemed relieved to see the girls.

"I'm taking Maisie to see you-know-what,"
Alice said mysteriously, and the cook whisked
several little packets into a wicker basket and
handed it to Alice to take with her. "Don't
spoil your lunch, Miss Alice," she added,
beaming.

"Where are we going?" Maisie asked,
as Alice pattered down one of the paths.
For a London garden, Alice's was huge, with

15

several enormous old trees, a rose terrace and a fish pool with a fountain.

"You'll see! Oh, and don't let Eddie go after the goldfish, Maisie, he'll fall in!"

Maisie hurried over to the pool, where Eddie seemed to be considering trying to walk on the lily pads, and scooped him up. Then she chased after her friend.

Close to the high stone wall at the end of the garden stood a giant tree, an oak, Maisie thought, though she wasn't certain. Trees were not something she had studied. *Although I probably should do*, Maisie decided, frowning to herself. She was quite sure that her hero, the great detective Gilbert Carrington, would be able to identify a tree from just a fragment of leaf. And who was to say it wouldn't be a vital clue in an investigation of her own, one of these days?

"Look!" Alice squeaked, pointing excitedly up into the tree.

Maisie peered among the new green leaves and gasped. High up in the branches was a tiny house, perfect and painted white. It looked like something out of a fairy tale.

"There are steps, you see," Alice explained. She pulled Maisie by the hand up the little staircase built around the trunk, and Eddie scampered after them. "There! Isn't it lovely?"

Maisie gazed at the little room, her eyes wide. It reminded her of Alice's doll's house – the way that everything was so small. Except this doll's house had a table and chairs they could sit on, and a real little stove with a shiny copper kettle on it. It was the prettiest toy she had ever seen.

"Of course, it's rather sad that I have to go away just when it's finished," Alice sighed. "But in the summer, when Papa and Miss Darling – Mama, I mean – when they're back, then it will be lovely…"

She sounded sad, and Maisie patted her hand. "Perhaps you'll be able to invite your friends from school here," she suggested.

"Maybe. They all sound so stiff and grand, those Honourables. Not fun like you, Maisie. Oh, what if I hate it?" Alice clutched Maisie's hands, her eyes filling with tears.

"You won't," Maisie told her firmly. "But if you do, I'll come and help, somehow. Your papa said I can visit, didn't he? They won't let me come every day, I shouldn't think, but you can send for me. You can … ummm … hang a signal out of your window!"

Maisie's last case had been a series of daring art thefts, and the gang had been caught when Maisie cracked the signal code they were using, which involved next door's washing line. Admittedly, she had thought she was solving a mystery about stolen washing, and she'd come across the art thefts almost accidentally, but she had still managed to identify the thieves!

"Oh yes!" Alice nodded excitedly. "Then it would be like a real adventure! Papa told me my sitting room will have a nice view of Russell Square. If I need you I shall hang out my blue bonnet, the one that tickles my ears. I never wear it. It's a very bright blue – you couldn't miss it. Do you promise you'll watch for it? The school isn't *all* that far from here, but it's a long way, over to Bloomsbury, if you're walking..."

Maisie shrugged. "I'm used to running errands, it won't matter. You only think it's a long walk because you go everywhere in your carriage, or your papa takes you in a hansom cab! Don't worry, Alice. I can come past every day, if you like."

Alice hugged her. "Oh, Maisie, that does make me feel better. Even if I don't see you, I shall know you've been to check that I'm all right. My own personal detective!"

"Gran, can I go and visit Alice at school? She's been there two weeks now, and I promised I'd go and see her. I'd have liked to go before, but Alice said the school doesn't allow too many visitors, in case the girls get homesick."

"I don't like the thought of you going over that way," Gran murmured, as she peeled potatoes over the sink. "Mr Lacey may think it's good enough for Miss Alice, but I wouldn't send you to a school there, Maisie."

"I wouldn't like to guess how many guineas that school costs," Maisie giggled. "It's an *Academy for Young Ladies*, if you please. I don't think the lodgers' rent would stretch to it, Gran."

"Don't remind me." Gran sighed. "We still haven't let that second-floor room, remember.

We're watching the pennies. But even if that school is dear, I don't like to think of Miss Alice near those rough, dirty places. Russell Square may be smart, but it's far too close to some very unsavoury streets. You're not to go near Seven Dials, Maisie, do you hear me? Murders and all sorts happen round there."

"I won't, Gran, I promise. I know about the murders – Gilbert Carrington solved a most awful bloodthirsty murder, don't you remember? When there was a foot left in the bottom of the stove!"

Gran put her hand to her mouth in horror, and Maisie realized she wasn't actually doing her own argument much good. "Besides," she added hurriedly, "it isn't even on the way."

Gran sniffed, as though she thought the dreadful Seven Dials might act like a magnet for someone as nosy as Maisie. She didn't really approve of Maisie's detecting habits.

"I've finished all my jobs now, Gran. Please can I go?" Maisie begged. "Alice said in her letter that I could come any time this afternoon."

"Oh, I suppose so. Do you know how to get there?"

Maisie nodded, trying not to smile. Gran didn't know that Maisie had walked past Miss Prenderby's Academy every day for the last two weeks, just as she had promised Alice. But she hadn't been anywhere near Seven Dials. Gran was right. The difference between smart Russell Square and the narrow, dirty streets only a few minutes closer to the river was shocking. Even Eddie thought they smelled bad.

Russell Square itself was lovely, Maisie thought, as she and Eddie walked past the fenced gardens. The houses were tall and much smarter than those in Albion Street. Miss Prenderby's house was not one of the largest, but it still looked grand to her. Little iron balconies, with pots of flowers standing on them, ran along the glittering windows.

She and Eddie walked up the freshly whitened steps which led to the double front door. By the side of the door was a glowing brass plate, which read *Miss Prenderby's Academy for Young Ladies of Quality*.

It was all a bit daunting, and Maisie began to wish that she hadn't brought Eddie with her. He was sitting next to her on the top step, giving his ears a good scratch. He did not look like the sort of dog who visited young ladies of quality.

But she had been invited, Maisie reminded herself firmly. She banged the shiny brass door knocker firmly, and smiled at the maid who came to answer it. "Miss Lacey, please. She's expecting me."

"Oh…" The maid, who wasn't all that much older than Maisie, looked doubtful about this. And particularly doubtful about Eddie. "What name shall I say then?"

"Maisie. Maisie Hitchins." Maisie did her best to ignore the way the girl was looking her up and down, and went on smiling politely.

"You'd better follow me…" the maid started to say, but she was interrupted by a delighted yelp that echoed through the dark entryway. She stepped back hurriedly, as Alice flung herself down the stairs and hugged Maisie.

"Miss Alice…" the maid murmured, beckoning Maisie in hurriedly. "You'll have

Miss Prenderby complaining. Get inside, do."

Several other girls popped their heads
round a door down the hallway and stared.
Maisie could hear them whispering.

"Who's she?"

"Is she a new pupil?"

"Of course she isn't! Look at the state of
her *dress*!"

This last comment was followed by a
chorus of giggles, and Maisie went pink and

tried to pretend she hadn't heard. There was no point telling these posh girls what she thought of them, and getting herself thrown out before she'd even had the chance to speak to Alice.

"Just ignore them, stupid little gossips," Alice said crossly. "Come up to my rooms, Maisie. Lizbeth, may we have tea, please." She swept Maisie away towards the stairs, glaring at the girls still nosying round the door.

Alice seemed to have grown bolder, Maisie thought, smiling to herself. She hadn't been used to spending time with other girls at all, but now she was holding her own. Maisie stared back at the girls as they went past, noting in surprise that the littlest of them looked no more than five years old. Who on earth would send such a tiny child away to school? Even a very smart school...

"Forget the dress, just look at that dog," someone sniggered, and Maisie whipped round to see the oldest of the girls smirking at her. A very tall, pretty girl, older than Maisie and Alice, but not by much. She had glossy black ringlets, and her dress was very smart, with a lace collar. Maisie disliked her at once.

"Ignore Bella, she's horridly rude," Alice said quite clearly, pulling Maisie away and up the stairs. "Come on, Eddie darling. You shall have a biscuit." She glowered at the dark-haired girl as she said it.

"Are they all like that?" Maisie asked in dismay, as she followed Alice into her pretty sitting room. Snowflake stood up on the armchair and hissed furiously at Eddie.

"No, it's really only Bella, but some of the others copy her. Though she's mean to them too, half the time." Alice sighed. "Ow, Snowflake! Don't scratch. You know quite well you don't like Eddie, you'll be much better off in my bedroom." She shooed the kittens in too, and closed the door. "Most of the girls are perfectly nice, though I do miss having someone as sensible as you to talk to, Maisie. People make the most dreadful fuss about things here."

"What sort of things?" Maisie asked

curiously, but they were interrupted by a quiet knock on the door, and a girl their own age backed her way in with the tea tray.

"Oh, this is Florence!" Alice sprang up to clear books off the little table. "Florence, this is my friend Maisie."

Florence put the tray down, and bobbed a curtsey to Maisie, which made her feel quite strange. She wasn't used to being curtseyed at.

"Florence, what's the matter?" Alice asked worriedly. The girl's nose was bright pink, and her cheeks were wet. She wrung her hands together, and then dabbed at her face with her apron. She looked exhausted, and so thin, Maisie thought.

"Nothing, Miss," Florence whispered. "Just Miss Bella. She made me spill the milk, Miss. I'm sorry, I'll go and fetch some more."

"Oooohh! That girl!" Alice said furiously. "I wish I could slap her, Florence, I really do."

Florence smiled at her. "Don't you dare, Miss Alice. It's very kind of you, but you'll get in trouble. Oh, and Miss Amaryllis says have you seen her best dancing slippers?" she added. "They've disappeared, and she's making ever such a commotion about them."

"She probably just put them down somewhere and forgot," Alice suggested, but she looked worried. "I don't mind the milk, Florence, we'll manage with what there is. You'll be in trouble if you go back for more, won't you?"

"Yes, Miss. Thank you, Miss," Florence said, backing out gratefully.

"Poor thing," Alice muttered. "She's an orphan. She came here just before I did from the Foundling Hospital and she has to work so hard."

"What was that about Miss Amaryllis?" Maisie asked.

Alice frowned. "She's the girl who has the next room. Can't you hear her?"

Maisie listened. Someone next door was stomping about, and wailing, and quite possibly throwing things.

"I'll go and see if she's all right in a minute, but I might let her calm down a bit first."

"Does she lose things a lot?" Maisie asked, wincing at a particularly loud crash.

Alice frowned. "Things are always disappearing here. Gloves. Dancing shoes. A gold bracelet. Some of the girls say there's a thief, which would be ever so exciting. But Miss Prenderby says it's just that we're all dreadfully spoilt and careless and don't look after our nice things."

Maisie pricked up her ears. She couldn't picture a thief somewhere like this. How could such rich, pampered little girls possibly need to steal anything?

"If there is a thief, then I think it's probably the dancing master," Alice said, sipping her tea thoughtfully. "He says he's French, but he doesn't sound anything like Madame Lorimer. And he has suspicious eyebrows."

Maisie laughed so much she snorted tea out of her nose, and made Eddie bark at her worriedly.

"What?" Alice asked, passing her a napkin. "Really, Maisie, that's not at all ladylike."

"Sorry… It was just … suspicious eyebrows!" Maisie sniggered.

"Well, I suppose it is a little bit funny," Alice admitted. "But you've not seen them, Maisie. A man with eyebrows like that could do anything."

Chapter Two

The girls at the Academy were clearly rich, Maisie thought to herself a few days later as she walked towards Russell Square to make sure that Alice hadn't hung out her bonnet. But that didn't mean they were happy. Even with Gran worrying about money, and the *Room to let* notice in the window starting to curl at the edges, Maisie didn't envy them.

Just before Maisie had left on her last visit, Amaryllis had burst into Alice's room in tears. She had then been joined by two of the littlest girls, Lucie and Arabel, complaining that Bella had pulled their hair. Alice had fussed over them and given them bonbons, and they'd gone away smiling, but Maisie wasn't sure that so many girls in the one house was a good idea. And she suspected that Miss Prenderby was right – unfortunately for Maisie's career as a detective. There wasn't a thief, just a lot of silly girls who were too thoughtless to take care of their things.

Still, at least Alice seemed to have settled in. She had an ally in Florence, the maid, and the younger girls seemed to think that she was their protector already. In fact, Alice probably didn't really need Maisie to look out for her at all, but she had promised.

So Maisie was rather surprised, when she walked up the side of the square towards Miss Prenderby's, to see something blue dangling over the pretty iron balcony. She let out a gasp and sped up, half running towards the school. It was definitely Alice's bonnet, she saw as she came closer.

Maisie halted on the other side of the road and looked up at the school worriedly. She had walked past late the previous afternoon, and there had most definitely been no bonnet. And it was only the middle of the morning now. Hopefully the signal hadn't been showing for all that long. Whatever could be the matter? Perhaps it was that suspicious dancing master? Maybe he really had been stealing things. Or Bella had been horrible again. But Maisie didn't think that Alice would summon her just for that. Surprisingly, she seemed to be quite good at dealing with the bullying older girl and her hangers-on. And Alice actually appeared to like having other people to fuss over for a change.

She crossed the road, and stood hesitating at the bottom of the gleaming stone steps. When she and Alice had thought up the signal, they hadn't discussed how Maisie was to answer it. She hadn't been invited, and she wasn't sure if the maids would just let her in. But there wasn't a lot else she could do… She trod determinedly up the steps and rang the bell.

The door was opened by Lizbeth the maid, who looked Maisie up and down just as doubtfully as before.

"Please can I see Miss Alice?" Maisie asked, hoping that Alice wasn't in a lesson, or something like that. She might well be wandering about with a book on her head. She'd told Maisie they had to do that for "deportment", which seemed to mean standing up straight.

Lizbeth shook her head and started to close the door, but Maisie caught it before she could. "Please! I'll wait, if she's busy. Alice wants to see me!"

Lizbeth sighed. "Does she now? Look, you can't see her because she isn't here. No one knows where she is." Then she looked panicked. "And don't tell anybody I said so! I'll get in trouble!"

Maisie hesitated for a moment, then she shoved the door open properly and marched in, squashing Lizbeth against the wall. "What do you mean you don't know where Alice is? You're supposed to be looking after her!"

"She's disappeared." Lizbeth shook her head, frowning worriedly. "No one's seen her since breakfast. She didn't turn up for her Italian lesson, so Miss Fleet, one of the teachers, went to fetch her. But she isn't anywhere. Not a sign of her."

"So, she's been gone all morning?" Maisie

asked. "And no one knows where?"

Lizbeth nodded. "She might have been
taken!" she said dramatically.

Usually, Maisie wouldn't have thought someone disappearing for a morning was all that important – it really wasn't very long. But this was Alice – she never went anywhere on her own. And then there was the signal, even though the teachers didn't know about that, of course.

"There's ink splashed all over the schoolroom floor," Lizbeth whispered. "Signs of a struggle, I reckon. And Miss Alice's father, he's very rich, isn't he? She's been taken for ransom, that's what I think. Though don't you tell anybody I said so!" she added quickly.

"Has anyone called the police?" Maisie asked. She didn't have a very good opinion of the police – an undercover policeman had been the last person to occupy their second-floor room and his policing had not been up to much – but they were better than nothing.

"Miss Prenderby doesn't want to yet," Lizbeth explained, glancing nervously towards the drawing room, which was Miss Prenderby's office. "It wouldn't be very good for the school, to have the police in. And she thinks Miss Alice is just homesick. She's sent Miss Fleet off to check at her house. Now, look, you'd better go, I'll get told off for letting you in."

"I'm not going!" Maisie snapped. "You've just lost my best friend!"

"Why ever is the front door open, Lizbeth?" A young, pink-faced lady, her hair trailing out in wisps from under her hat, came hurrying up the front steps.

Lizbeth rolled her eyes, and shut the door, with Maisie and Eddie on the inside.

"Any sign of her, Miss?" the maid asked hopefully.

"No, none!" Miss Fleet said breathlessly. "And it was dreadfully embarrassing, trying not to admit that Miss Alice has disappeared. I'm sure the servants suspect that something is wrong. I had to make up a story about her going off with a friend. The butler looked at me like I was a lunatic."

Maisie sniffed. She had met that butler.

"Who is this?" Miss Fleet asked, noticing Maisie.

"She's a friend of Miss Alice. Come to see her, and found her – well, missing."

"Oh my goodness!" Miss Fleet wailed, collapsing on to a little velvet chair. "What are we going to do? I'm sure she's been kidnapped, and her father is so very well known in business. It'll be the end of us, it really will!"

"Sophia, calm down!" An icy voice snapped Miss Fleet back to her senses at once, and even Maisie felt herself straighten up. Eddie crept quietly behind her legs to hide.

Miss Prenderby had come out of the drawing room, and was eyeing them all through a pair of gold-rimmed spectacles. She was tall and very thin, so thin that her face was bony, and her nose looked knife-sharp.

"And you are?" she asked Maisie coldly.

Maisie curtseyed. She didn't actually intend to – her knees did it without being told. "I'm Maisie Hitchins, Miss. I'm a friend of Miss Alice. I came to visit last week, and she – er – asked me to visit again today." That was sort of true, anyway...

"Do you have any idea where she is?" Miss Prenderby asked sharply.

"No!" Maisie shook her head. "But I shouldn't think she's run away, Miss. She was enjoying herself when I saw her last week. It was different for her, but she said she liked it here. She had made friends."

"You see! She must have been kidnapped!" Miss Fleet wailed again.

"Piffle!" snapped Miss Prenderby. "You, Miss Hitchins, come with me. As you know Miss Lacey well, perhaps you can shed some light on where she might have gone."

She sailed away down the corridor, and Maisie and Eddie scurried after her, with Miss Fleet tottering behind. Maisie had expected that they would go up to Alice's rooms – perhaps to see if she had packed a bag. But instead, Miss Prenderby glided into a large room with desks and chairs, and a blackboard.

"The young ladies are having a dancing lesson, thankfully," she explained to Maisie. "We can't carry on lessons in here until all this has been cleared away."

This was a large puddle of black ink, from one of the ink wells, spilled across the desk and down on to the tiled floor. Wet little black pawprints led out across the tiles in a delicate pattern, and Maisie sucked in a breath through her teeth. That was going to be a pain to clean, she thought. Spirits of vinegar might get it off, perhaps, but she wouldn't count on it. Then she clicked her tongue irritably. She hadn't had a case to solve for too long – how could she even think about tidying away such an important clue?

She stooped down to examine the mess – lots of paw prints, some tiny, and a few larger ones. The kittens, she thought, as well as Snowflake. And there were several long smears, as though in the end the cats had been pulled away.

"Miss Alice was in here just after breakfast. I saw her myself," Miss Prenderby explained. "She was practising her French vocabulary. But no one has seen her since."

"All that ink! As though there had been a struggle!" Miss Fleet bleated. "I really do think we should call the police, Miss Prenderby!"

Miss Prenderby drew back her shoulders and seemed to grow even taller for a moment, and then she sighed. "Perhaps. The child has been missing for two hours now. I was quite sure she had simply gone home. She is unused to school, after all."

Eddie sniffed cautiously at the ink and eyed the trail of paw prints. Maisie took a tighter grasp on his lead – she really didn't want him chasing Alice's cats in front of the icy Miss Prenderby.

Then she frowned. No white cats had emerged from behind the curtains to tease Eddie. There were no hissing little furballs stalking along the bookshelf. Snowflake very much disliked Eddie and took every chance she could to spit at him, and she'd taught her kittens to do the same. So why wasn't she here now, having a stand-off with her old enemy?

"Miss Prenderby, where are the cats?" Maisie asked, looking around.

The headmistress shuddered. "In Miss Alice's rooms, I suppose."

"Are you sure?" Maisie looked doubtfully at the pattern of paw prints. "They didn't walk out of the classroom, did they? The prints stop here. Someone carried them away, and I wouldn't have thought even Alice could carry all three of them at once."

"Oh no, they weren't in her room when I went to look for her," Miss Fleet said, shaking her head.

"I thought they were down here, Miss," Lizbeth put in, from the doorway. "You know how the little girls like to give them bits of their breakfast."

"So they're gone too," Maisie said. "Well, a kidnapper wouldn't bother to take three white cats with them, would they?" She looked thoughtfully at the inky trail again. She couldn't tell exactly what it meant, but she was having serious doubts about this whole kidnapping theory.

Chapter Three

Miss Prenderby stared at Maisie, and her eyebrows went into perfect arches. "Indeed a kidnapper wouldn't…" she murmured. "Lizbeth, go and check Miss Alice's rooms again, see if the basket those animals came in is missing."

"And her coat," Maisie suggested. "If one of her coats is gone, that doesn't seem much like a kidnap either, does it?"

"Of course." Miss Prenderby nodded, and Lizbeth raced off upstairs. "Sophia, are you quite certain the girl hasn't just gone home?"

"I asked!" Miss Fleet protested. "But it was rather difficult, Miss Prenderby, when we didn't want to alarm the servants…"

"Hmph," was all Miss Prenderby said, but she allowed herself a tiny smile when Lizbeth came galloping back to say that the basket was missing from the bottom of Miss Alice's wardrobe, and her best coat with the velvet collar had gone too. "Just as I thought," she murmured. "The silly child has run off home."

"But why?" Miss Fleet asked. "She was happy here! And more to the point, she isn't *at* home. I still think we should call the police. What if something has happened to her?"

Miss Prenderby frowned. "I very much

doubt that they will be any use. But if Miss Alice has not returned by lunchtime, we will call them." Then she stalked out, with Miss Fleet hurrying after her.

Maisie was left in the schoolroom with Lizbeth the maid, who looked depressed.

"Do *you* still think she's been kidnapped?" Maisie asked her thoughtfully.

"Well, maybe not…" Lizbeth sighed. "Lot of nonsense that Miss Fleet talks. She's gone off for a jaunt, I should think. Fancied a day out!"

"And taken the cats?" Maisie said doubtfully. "Besides, I don't think Alice would. She isn't used to going out on her own."

Lizbeth shrugged. "Look, all I know is I've got to clean up this mess before the young ladies finish their dancing. So if you don't mind…"

Maisie nodded. Perhaps she could go

and look around the nearby streets, she thought. And ask if anyone had seen Alice. She understood that Miss Prenderby didn't want to call the police – it would cause gossip about the school – but she didn't like the idea of waiting around and doing nothing. She was just turning to leave, thinking she'd let herself out and not bother Lizbeth, who was on her knees looking at the puddle of ink, when she heard the girl let out an enormous sigh.

"Of all the days for them to sack Florence…" Lizbeth muttered.

"What?" Maisie gasped.

"Florence. They sent her packing. So we're short-handed. How'm I going to get all this done, and the bedrooms too?"

"Why? What happened?" Maisie asked. She had liked poor, frightened little Florence, even after a few minutes, and Alice had obviously been friendly with her.

"Miss Prenderby said she was stealing." Lizbeth wrinkled her nose. "I don't reckon she was, poor little mite. She wasn't bright enough, or brave enough, I'd say. But Miss Bella threw a right tantrum about her best kid gloves, threatened to write to her parents, you see. So Florence got dismissed. No reference either. It all happened last night, but at least they didn't send her out in the dark. She left after breakfast this morning."

Maisie frowned. "But … where did she go?

Alice said she'd come from the Foundling Hospital."

Lizbeth shrugged. "Went back to it, I suppose. Now, if you don't mind, I've got to fetch a scrubbing brush and clean this floor." And she hurried out, leaving Maisie staring after her.

"I don't know if places like that take you back, once you've left and got a job," Maisie murmured to Eddie. "Poor Florence. She could be out on the streets, all on her own…" Then she stared at him, so silently and for so long that Eddie let out a worried whine.

"Sorry," Maisie whispered. "But Eddie, what if Florence isn't on her own? What if Alice went with her?"

Maisie trailed slowly down the front steps of the school, wondering how to start looking for Alice and Florence. She was almost sure that they were together. Alice had been so keen to have an adventure of her own, and she would have been furious about Florence's dismissal.

But if they weren't at Alice's house, as Miss Fleet said, then where were they? Maisie was sure that the Laceys' servants wouldn't have lied to Miss Fleet. And she supposed that if Alice had turned up at her house, they would have had to send her back to school. So Alice couldn't be there. *Could she possibly have gone to Albion Street?* Maisie thought, dithering on the pavement. It would be just typical if she had come to look for Alice here, and all the while Alice was at home, looking for her.

"Where else, Eddie?" she wondered. "Alice doesn't have any relations, she told me so when I visited. Oh!"

Eddie yelped in surprise.

"Sorry, sorry! But the tree house, Eddie!
I'm sure Alice must know a secret place to
climb over her garden wall. That must be
where they're hiding!"

It seemed such a perfect solution, Maisie
thought to herself proudly. And it would
explain why the servants hadn't seen Alice,
and had told Miss Fleet she wasn't at home.
All the while she and Florence had been
hidden away in the garden!

"We'd better go and see if they're all right,"
Maisie told Eddie, setting off around the
square. "I wonder how Alice knew the way? It
isn't all that far, I suppose. Her house is closer
to here than Albion Street. But she isn't used
to wandering around London like we are."

She quickened her step a little. She was

sure that the tree house was where Alice and Florence had been heading. But she didn't know if they had got there safely. It was all guesswork, and the two of them could quite easily be lost somewhere. Alice had been fussed over and babied since the day she was born – she wasn't used to finding her way around, not at all. And Florence was a foundling, in her first job as a servant. She probably didn't even know where Russell Square was, let alone anywhere else.

The two of them could be anywhere by now, Maisie thought anxiously. *How could they have found their way safely home?*

Maisie hurried along the edge of the square, wondering which way Alice and Florence would have gone. Would anyone have noticed them, perhaps? Two young girls, lugging a basket – a basket that was probably yowling. Perhaps someone would remember. But Russell Square was so quiet and respectable. The only children playing in the garden were accompanied by a uniformed nanny, and they were so clean they surely hadn't been out of doors for very long.

A hansom cab was rumbling slowly past her, the chestnut horse lifting his feet wearily.

Maisie stopped dead, and stared at the heavily muffled driver. Perhaps Alice had taken a cab? She hardly ever walked, and she probably had money that her papa had given her.

"Are you lost, dearie?" The cabbie was leaning over from his seat at the back of the cab. "You're about the same age as my little girl, you know. I wouldn't want to see her wandering around looking that worried."

Maisie smiled up at him. "Thank you, but I'm not lost, I'm looking for my friends. I think *they* could be lost though, that's why I looked worried. Neither of them knows their way around London." Maisie sighed. "I don't know where to start," she admitted. "I don't suppose you were round here earlier this morning and saw them?" she asked, though she knew it wasn't likely. "Two girls, about the same age as me, with a basket?"

"Sorry, Missie." He shook his head. "But what are they doing traipsing round the streets anyway?" he asked. Maisie almost smiled. He sounded so disapproving, just like Gran.

"They're from the school, over there." Maisie pointed. "I think my friend Alice is trying to get home."

"Homesick, eh, poor thing?" The cabbie snorted, and the ends of his fat grey moustache flew up in the air. "I wouldn't want to send our Ellen away. You hop in the cab, Missie, and your dog. We'll nip over to the shelter, see if anyone's seen your friends."

"The shelter?" Maisie frowned.

"Cabmen's shelter. Over by Hanover Square, the nearest one. We'll see who's around. I can get a quick mug of tea at the same time, and it'll give old Joey here a bit of a rest."

"Oh!" Maisie nodded gratefully. "Thank you!" The hansom cab drivers were probably the best possible people to ask, and now she'd get to talk to several of them at once. Russell Square was quite smart, and there might well have been cabs going past when

Alice and Florence had left the school.

The cab was an old one, and a bit battered – it rattled as it bumped over the paving stones, but the brasswork shone, and the cabbie whistled to himself as they drove through the streets. They pulled up at the side of the Hanover Square garden, in a line of cabs by a small bright green building, and the cabbie tied up Joey, and helped Maisie and Eddie down. Then he popped his head around the door of the shelter, and called, "Mug of tea, please, Fred. And anyone seen two little girls wandering round Russell Square way?"

"They had a basket," Maisie added, peering curiously into the tiny room, which was filled with a steamy tea and toast scented fug, and crammed with men in bowler hats. "With three cats in it."

One of the men looked up from his sandwich and snorted with laughter. "I saw them – halfway down Southampton Row. Three cats, was it? I'd have guessed at least ten of the beasts. Claws and paws sticking out of that basket every which way, there was."

"Oh, when was that, please?" Maisie asked eagerly.

The man frowned. "Just after the fussy old lady. Before the courting couple. About ten o'clock, it must have been."

Maisie looked up at the clock on the wall – it was nearly eleven o'clock. Alice and Florence could have got a good way further on by now. But at least she knew that they were together. And it sounded as though the cats were making them easy to spot. If she went to Southampton Row, there was a good chance that someone else would remember which way the girls with the struggling cats had gone.

The driver took another bite of sandwich, and chewed it slowly. "They looked upset, come to think of it. I just thought it was because of the cats making a nuisance of themselves. But the little blonde one, she was looking up at the street sign, as if they were lost..."

"Oh dear," Maisie murmured.

The friendly cabbie who'd brought her gulped down his tea and grinned. "Wanting a lift to Southampton Row, are you then?"

Maisie went pink. "Oh no, I wasn't going to ask..."

"Come on, Missie. I know you weren't. I want to make sure you find them. But be careful, you hear?" He frowned as he passed back his mug, and led her to the cab. "Maybe you ought to ask a constable."

Maisie shook her head. "I'm not sure the police would listen. They haven't been gone that long, you see. But I'm worried they might've got lost…"

"Can't be too careful, round that way," the cabbie muttered. "Just don't go chasing off anywhere nasty."

"I won't," Maisie assured him, as she climbed back into the cab. She was almost sure he wouldn't be fussing like this if she were a boy… But then he probably wouldn't have stopped to help her either, so there were some advantages to being a girl detective after all.

Chapter Four

Southampton Row led into Holborn, and
a maze of tiny streets. It was not quite as
disreputable as Seven Dials, but it wasn't far
off, and Maisie and Eddie stood uncertainly
on the corner of Little Queen Street. There
were rumours that all these narrow lanes
were to be demolished to make way for a
brand new road, and Maisie couldn't help

thinking it was a good idea. Piles of rubbish lay about – and a couple of ragged children were picking through them, looking for things they could sell to the rag merchants. Maisie was unusual enough here, in her clean dress and good boots. Alice would look like a visitor from another world.

Maisie gulped nervously – Gran had told her so many times to stay out of places like this. But even Gran wouldn't expect her to leave Alice and Florence here. Of course, they could just have turned into Oxford Street – Alice might even know her way. She had probably been there with one of her governesses, or out for a treat with her father, as the road was famous for its shops. And although it was a longish route back to Alice's house, it was a perfectly sensible one.

But Maisie had a worried feeling in the pit of her stomach. Alice had gone wandering off looking for an adventure, and Maisie suspected that she might have found one.

"What d'*you* want?" demanded the grubby little girl stirring the rubbish across the street. "Standing about staring!"

"I'm looking for someone," Maisie told her.

"Two someones. Girls about my age, with a basket?"

"Oh, them," the ragged girl sneered. "They went with Ma Hanson."

"You saw them?" Maisie was so excited that her voice came out as a squeak, and the little girl sniggered.

"Course we saw them!" She nudged the even dirtier little boy who'd come to see what was going on. "Those two who had the cats!"

He snorted. "They won't have them now, will they? Those cats'll be trimming someone's opera cloak. Nice bit of white fur. Kitten mittens!" He giggled, as though this was the best joke he'd heard in ages.

Maisie stared at them in horror. Snowflake and her little kittens! Fur mittens! "Alice would never let anyone do that," she murmured.

"She won't have had a choice," the girl

76

pointed out. "They were lost, and Ma Hanson said she'd help them. Well, so she will. For a price."

Maisie glared disgustedly at the two children, and they glared back. She was on their turf, and Maisie sensed they didn't want to help her. "Where is she then, this Ma Hanson?" she asked coaxingly. "I've got a penny."

The ragged girl folded her arms. "Sixpence."

Maisie knew she could probably make a better bargain, but she didn't have time to argue. "Here." She rooted in her pocket. "And I don't have any more, so don't bother asking," she added hurriedly.

The little boy darted at her, ready to snatch the coin, but Maisie held it up out of his reach. "Oh no, you don't. Not till you show me where to find Ma Hanson."

"Come on then," he growled, and the two
of them scuttled off down the alley, looking
back scornfully as Maisie picked her way
through the dirt. They led her through a maze
of grubby little streets, while Maisie hurried
after them, glancing around her and trying to
remember landmarks. She didn't have another
sixpence to pay them to bring her back.

HANSON'S

"Here! Ma Hanson's is over there. Now give us the money," the girl snapped, holding out her greyish hand. When Maisie dropped the coin into it, the two of them made off as fast as they could, as though they thought she might try to go back on the bargain.

Maisie looked around nervously. The alley was empty, but she still felt as though she was being watched. Perhaps it was only rats, but that didn't make her feel much better. Eddie pressed nervously against her legs, and whined.

Across the alley was a dirty, crooked little shop, its window a patchwork of cracked and filthy glass. Written in shaky painted letters above the window was *Hanson's*. It was impossible to tell what the shop sold, but Maisie suspected that whatever it was, she didn't want it.

Maisie was just readying herself to march inside when a thin, high wail echoed out across the street. She gasped. What was Ma Hanson doing to Alice and Florence in there?

Eddie barked furiously, and they dashed across the alley. Maisie flung open the creaking door, and the pair of them half fell into the shop.

"Maisie!" Alice shrieked. "Help!" She was clutching the cat basket, trying to tug it away from a red-faced woman who was swathed in about six different dresses and shawls, wrapped around her in layers like a jam roly-poly. The woman was a lot stronger than Alice, and Alice was only just managing to keep hold of the basket.

"Give it here, you silly brat," Ma Hanson panted. "Those cats are mine now!"

"I won't!" Alice shrieked back, with a

fierce tug. "You shan't have them!"

Maisie saw a furious white furry face
pop out from under the lid of the basket.
The straps that held it closed were obviously
coming undone.

She hurried forward to help Alice, and saw that Florence was curled in a ball by the counter, a red mark across her face. Someone had slapped her!

"Where did you come from?" Ma Hanson snapped angrily at Maisie, and Eddie growled. He was only little, but he didn't really understand that, and he didn't like people raising their voices at Maisie. He let out a stream of fierce, sharp barks, and darted at the fat woman's ankles.

The three cats yowled loudly inside the carrier. They'd been stuffed into a tight basket, shaken about, shouted at, and now that dratted dog had turned up. They'd had enough. Snowflake burst out from under the lid, meowing furiously, and scratched all five of her claws down Ma Hanson's face, from eyebrow to chin. She was followed by her hissing, spitting kittens.

"Run!" Maisie cried, reaching down to grab Florence's arm and haul her up.

Ma Hanson had fallen back against the counter, shrieking words that Maisie really hoped Alice wouldn't remember, but Maisie didn't think Ma Hanson would be down for long. Pushing Alice in front of her, she yanked the door open, and the three of them fled into the street, trailed by three white cats and a very over-excited dog…

Leading the way, Maisie raced as far as Oxford Street before she dared to slow down and look behind her. They'd been going so fast that she hadn't even looked at her landmarks. It was amazing what pure fear could do for one's sense of direction.

No one seemed to be following them, thank goodness. Ma Hanson had been screaming blue murder, but they had managed to run fast enough to leave her behind.

Alice was clutching both the kittens, one tucked under each arm. Snowflake was darting after them, occasionally hissing at Eddie, who scampered along between Maisie and Florence. At last, Maisie darted into a little back street, her sides heaving, and leaned against the wall. Florence sank down on to a wooden crate that had been left on the pavement, and Alice leaned next to Maisie, still clutching the wriggling kittens.

"We should have grabbed the basket," she murmured.

"You shouldn't have gone in the first place!" Maisie snapped. "What were you thinking? Let alone Snowflake being made into fur trim, you and Florence weren't far off from turning into meat pie filling!"

"I'm sorry, Maisie," Alice said, her eyes filling with tears. "I hung out the signal for you, but there wasn't time. I had to do something. They turned Florence out into the street! She hadn't anywhere to go!"

Maisie sighed. "I know. I didn't mean to be cross. I was frightened for you. Please say you won't ever do that again! You should be safe at school."

Alice looked up, her eyes flashing. "I'm not going to go back there, Maisie. What's Florence meant to do?"

Maisie rolled her eyes. "So where are you going then? Miss Prenderby's already sent one of the teachers to your house. The wet one, what's her name?"

Even Florence sniggered at that description.

85

"Miss Fleet," she whispered.

"Yes. Her. So you can't go home. Besides, the servants would see you."

"I was going to hide us in the tree house," Alice said, in a small voice. "I have my allowance from Papa, it would last us a while."

"There's no water closet, Alice!" Maisie hissed.

Alice blinked. "I hadn't thought of that…"

"It isn't a thing young ladies think about," Maisie agreed.

"We'll have to find somewhere else then," Alice said determinedly. "Maisie – I don't suppose your gran would let us stay with you, would she?"

"Even if she did, the school are going to call the police if you're not back by lunchtime," Maisie pointed out. "And the police will telegraph your father."

"On his wedding journey!" Florence cried. "Oh, Miss Alice, you can't! You'll have to go back."

"But what about you?" Alice wailed.

"Actually," Maisie said thoughtfully. "I might have a plan…"

Chapter Five

Gran looked up from scrubbing Alice's inky fingers with a lemon-soaked cloth. "Rinse your hands in that bowl of hot water, Miss Alice, we've nearly got it all off." She looked over at Snowflake and the kittens, curled up in an old wooden crate by the kitchen stove. "But they'll have black feet for a while, Miss. I can't see them letting me wash their paws!"

She glanced at Florence, who was holding a damp cloth to her cheek where Ma Hanson had hit her. "So they just put you out into the street? A foundling child, with nowhere to go? I said I didn't like the idea of that school, Maisie, didn't I?"

"They said I was a thief. I didn't steal anything, but I spilled some gravy on one of the young ladies, ma'am," Florence said humbly. "And I did break some china."

"Only because one of the little ones left a doll on the stairs, Mrs Hitchins," Alice put in swiftly. "Florence is very careful, and beautifully trained. Aren't you?" she added, almost fiercely.

"But we don't need another maid," Gran sighed. "I'd like to help, but we're short a lodger, and that means I just can't afford to pay her, Miss Alice."

"She doesn't want paying, Gran," Maisie explained. "Just her board and lodging. A place to sleep. And – well, you might need her." She took a deep breath. This was the part of the plan that Gran was not going to like. "Gran, will you write me a reference, so I can go and ask for Florence's job? Alice is sure that someone else is stealing from the girls, and if I can find out who it is, they might give Florence her job back. She can sleep in my room and do my jobs while I'm at the school. And I'd be paid, Gran! You can't say the money wouldn't come in useful."

Gran looked at her thoughtfully. "It doesn't sound to me as though they treat the staff well in that place, Maisie. I'm not sure I want you working there." She sighed. "Though you're right, the money would certainly be handy."

Maisie blinked at her. She had expected
Gran to say no at once, and she'd been ready
to beg and plead and argue. Gran thought
of Maisie's detecting as just being nosy, and
she usually tried to discourage it as much
as possible.

A faint pink flush appeared across the tops of Gran's cheekbones, and she sniffed. "That Miss Barnes next door was very impressed with your last bit of detecting, Maisie. When you worked out why all that washing kept disappearing."

Maisie giggled. It was typical of Gran that solving the mystery of the washing would be more important than recovering thousands of pounds-worth of missing paintings.

"She said she was sure I was very proud of you," Gran murmured. "And I am... I just worry that you'll get yourself into something dangerous. And you did!"

It was quite true. One of the art thieves had caught Maisie following him. She sighed. She'd known that Gran would find that hard to forget.

"But I don't suppose you can get into that

much trouble in a school for young ladies. Oh, I do beg your pardon, an *Academy*…"

"You mean I can do it?" Maisie squeaked joyfully. "You'll write me a reference?"

"What is the world coming to?" Gran muttered. "Lying for my own granddaughter. Oh yes, I'll do it, Maisie. But you've got, let's see … two weeks, that's all. And I don't approve. False references!"

She approved even less when Maisie and Alice vanished upstairs to talk to Miss Lottie Lane, the actress who lived on the third floor. Maisie was going to need a disguise, so that no one at the school recognized her as Alice's friend. Gran had written the reference for her as Milly Tatham, which was the name of a girl who'd rented one of the upstairs rooms a long time ago, she said. Milly needed to look quite different from Maisie.

Even though Miss Lane was an actress, and Gran was always saying that she was flighty and unreliable, she was one of Maisie's greatest allies as a detective. She had a stock of useful clothes for disguises, and she'd shown Maisie how to use greasepaint too. Now she looked at Maisie thoughtfully.

"It shouldn't really be that difficult. After all, you still want to be a young girl. But I think it's harder to do that than it is to turn you into an old lady, or a delivery boy. Hmmmm… What would you say is the most noticeable thing about Maisie?" she asked Alice suddenly.

"Her hair?" Alice answered, gazing at Maisie with her head on one side. Maisie's hair was red and curly. It was hard to miss.

"Exactly. So we definitely have to deal with that. I suppose your gran would have forty fits if we dyed it?" she said to Maisie.

"I think she might faint," Maisie agreed.

"A wig then." Miss Lane opened a cupboard, humming happily to herself, and proceeded to lift out various hair pieces. "We can't go too far away from your natural colour, Maisie, or it'll look wrong. Brown, maybe. Or strawberry blonde. Try this, you'll see what I mean." She slipped a black wig over Maisie's own hair, tucking away the wispy bits, and brushed it into place.

Alice burst out laughing, and Maisie peered into the little hand mirror Miss Lane was holding out.

"Ugh!" she squeaked. The black wig made her look half-dead, like some dreadful vampire creature.

"You see," Miss Lane said, chuckling. "Now try this one." The next wig was a dark blonde, much closer to Maisie's own red hair, though still different enough.

Miss Lane eyed her thoughtfully as she tweaked and pulled. "Oh yes, much better," she purred. "Just a minute, Maisie." She seized a pencil out of her huge cosmetics case, and drew freckles over Maisie's cheeks and nose. "There!"

Maisie looked nervously into the mirror, and caught her breath in surprise. There was another girl looking back at her. It really was very odd.

"Would you recognize me?" she asked
Alice.

Alice frowned. "Well, I might. But only
because I know you. No one else at Miss
Prenderby's will." Then she glanced at the
little clock under the mirror and gasped. "It's
a quarter to one! We have to get back, before
Miss Prenderby decides to inform the police.
Let's go now, Maisie, come on!"

Gran had found an old wicker basket that
looked quite like the one the cats had been
carried away in, and the two girls set off back
to Russell Square, accompanied by furious
mewing.

Alice looked tired and rather shabby, with
greyish marks on her pretty muslin frock,
and dusty shoes. But then she needed to look

like she had been wandering the streets all morning.

Miss Fleet opened the front door, rather than one of the maids, which showed how Alice's disappearance had thrown the school into a flurry. She seemed to be about to tell them that whatever it was, she couldn't possibly deal with it now, when she noticed Alice and shrieked, "Oh, Alice! Where have you been?"

As Alice stepped into the hallway, all the girls in the house seemed to pop their heads round doors to stare. But then Miss Prenderby appeared, and they melted away as fast as they'd arrived.

"Alice. We have been very worried about you," Miss Prenderby said, her voice icy with disapproval.

Alice wilted, hanging her head, and Maisie

coughed politely.

"And you are?" Miss Prenderby enquired, still disapproving.

"Milly Tatham, ma'am. I found Miss Alice in Oxford Street. She was lost, poor thing. One of her kittens isn't well…"

"I thought he was missing home," Alice added, remembering her part in the story. "And that if we could just go there for a little while, it might perk him up. But then I couldn't quite remember the way, so I tried to come back to the school and I got so lost. This kind girl brought me back. I'm so sorry if I've worried you, Miss Prenderby." Then she added, "I hope you didn't telegraph my father, he'd be upset if he knew I'd got lost."

Miss Prenderby eyed her crossly, but Alice stared back looking innocent, and eventually the headmistress turned to Maisie.

"We are most grateful," she said, although she didn't really sound it.

"If you please, ma'am, is that clock right?" Maisie asked, staring worriedly at the grandfather clock in the corner of the hall.

"Five minutes slow," Miss Prenderby told her, raising one eyebrow.

"Oh…" Maisie sighed, and let her shoulders sag.

"Whatever's the matter?" Alice asked, and Maisie could see that she was trying not to giggle. Alice really was a terrible actress.

"It's nothing, Miss. Just that I was on my way to be interviewed for a job, when I found you. I'm too late to go back now. They'll have given it to someone else."

"Oh, what a pity," Alice sighed, and tried not to look too hopefully at Miss Prenderby.

"What sort of position were you seeking?" Miss Prenderby asked slowly.

"As a housemaid, ma'am. My previous lady, she's not well and she's going to live with her brother, so she's given all of us notice, you see. We're to leave as soon as we can."

"Do you have references?" Miss Prenderby asked.

Maisie pulled out a neatly folded letter

and handed it over.

Miss Prenderby read it, frowning. "It so happens that one of our maids has recently been dismissed. Hmm. You had better go and speak to the housekeeper. Take her downstairs, please, Miss Fleet."

Maisie managed one quick, delighted glance at Alice, before she hurried after Miss Fleet towards the servants' quarters. She could hear Miss Prenderby's chilly voice echoing after them as they went.

"Alice, would you carry those animals upstairs and release them, please. The screeching does not mix well with Marianne's flute practice…"

Chapter Six

Maisie had never realized before how lucky Sally, the maid at 31 Albion Street, really was. She had her own nice room, with a wash stand, a wardrobe and a comfortable iron bedstead, with good clean sheets, several blankets and a quilt.

At Miss Prenderby's, Maisie (who was trying very hard to think of herself as Milly) slept up in the attics, under the roof, next door to Lizbeth and the kitchen maid. The attics were freezing, even though it was April. And Lizbeth had told her that in the summer they were roasting hot. The tiny rooms were furnished with an odd mixture of cast offs, and the beds were dreadfully lumpy.

The housekeeper, Mrs Elkins, was quite nice, but the cook was horrible. Mrs Albert made delicious food, but the kitchen was not a pleasant place to be. Anyone who got in her way was likely to be thumped over the head with a ladle, and Lizbeth said that she had once bashed Luke, the boot boy, so hard with a colander that Luke ended up wearing it as a necklace. Maisie was not entirely sure that she believed this, but seeing Mrs Albert throwing a fit about burnt porridge that morning, she had almost been convinced.

The maids spent as much time as possible above stairs, trying to stay out of Mrs Albert's way. Maisie decided it was quite lucky that the pupils at the school were so untidy – it meant there was always something to clear up. It was also good because Maisie wanted to stay as close to the girls as possible, so she could be on the lookout for anything suspicious.

"Milly!" A small girl appeared in front of her, and Maisie frowned to herself, trying to remember which one she was. She looked only about five years old, so she must be Lucie – the baby of the school. Maisie thought back to the two little girls who had come in to see Alice on her first visit to the school. Yes, this was Lucie.

"Can I help you, Miss Lucie?" she said.

"I've torn my pinafore," the small girl whispered to her, seriously.

"Oh dear…"

"Will you mend it for me?" Lucie pleaded. "I'll get in trouble, otherwise."

Maisie nodded. It probably wasn't part of her job to mend the girls' clothes, but she'd finished dusting Miss Prenderby's china figurines and she would rather stay out of the kitchen. And it was only a straight tear in the little girl's cotton pinafore.

"My workbox is in the schoolroom," Lucie told her hopefully. "We all have to have one, but Miss Fleet says my sewing looks like a black beetle wandered across my work…"

"I'll come and sew it up," Maisie told her. "I'll sit in the window seat, and you tell me if you see Miss Fleet or Miss Prenderby coming, then I can duck behind the curtains."

Lucie giggled delightedly at this masterly plan, and on the way to the schoolroom she fetched two of her other little friends to help her stand guard. The girls had lessons in the morning, and mostly amused themselves in the afternoons with music practice, extra dancing lessons and ladylike things such as embroidery, so the schoolroom was empty. Maisie settled herself in the window seat, and started to stitch up the tear.

"Oh, you're very good," Clarissa told her admiringly, and Arabel agreed. "Tiny stitches. Better than Florence."

"Florence, was that the last maid? Did you get her to do your mending then?" Maisie asked, smiling.

"Yes, she was never mean to us. Lizbeth snaps sometimes, if we get in her way, but Florence was sweet."

"So why did she leave?" Maisie murmured, biting off a new length of thread.

The little girls looked at each other doubtfully, as if they weren't sure they were supposed to talk about it. Then Lucie leaned close to Maisie and whispered, "They said she was a thief. But I don't believe it! Florence was nice!"

"She was," Arabel agreed. "And she was always scared of Miss Prenderby, and even

Mrs Elkins the housekeeper. I don't think she'd have dared to steal anything! She was terrified of getting into trouble."

Maisie nodded. She had thought that too. "So what got stolen then?" she asked.

"My gold bracelet," Clarissa said, sadly. "It was on my dressing table, in its little box – and then it was gone. Miss Prenderby said I lost it, but I really didn't. Papa gave it to me, I took good care of it always."

"Lots of things. Marianne's best silk sash," Lucie added. "Frederica's silver hairbrush."

"But the day before yesterday, Bella's new kid gloves disappeared," Arabel explained, "and she made such a fuss! She said Florence had been in her room – and of course she had, it's her job to clean the rooms! But Bella swore she'd seen Florence poking about in her things. And Marianne and Frederica agreed with her.

So Miss Prenderby dismissed Florence."

Maisie shook her head. "Sounds like I'd better not get on the wrong side of Miss Bella."

"Oh no, don't!" Lucie agreed. "She's horrid. She's mean to us all the time."

"Because we're the littlest," Clarissa told her. "She shook you, didn't she, Arabel? When you spilled the milk at breakfast."

"But can't you tell someone?" Maisie asked, frowning.

Arabel shook her head. "No, because Bella is one of Miss Prenderby's favourites. She's been here for so long, and her mother and father are terribly rich. They send her lots of nice things. Bella gets shown off to all the parents of new girls, because she's so pretty and always has lovely dresses."

"But she never ever goes home," Clarissa pointed out. "Because her parents are in –

where is it? Vienna or Paris or somewhere. I wouldn't like that, even if they do send her all those presents. She even has to stay at the school at Christmas."

Maisie shivered. That did sound awful.

"What are you little ones doing gossiping in the corner?" someone asked nastily, and Arabel and Clarissa jumped backwards so quickly they ended up sitting on Maisie's lap. Maisie had been half hidden by the curtains anyway, in case any teachers came in, so now Bella couldn't see her at all.

"Nothing…" Lucie said, but her voice wobbled.

"Secrets, Lucie?" Bella purred. "I think I had better tell Miss Prenderby that you're plotting something."

"I'm not!" Lucie wailed. "I hate you, Bella! You're mean all the time, and no one likes you, so there!"

"You little cat!" Bella snapped, and she snatched one of Lucie's long curls, and yanked it, so that the little girl burst into tears.

"Leave her alone!" Maisie snapped, pushing the curtain aside and glaring at the older girl. "She's only little! And she didn't do anything to you."

"She's a rude, ill-mannered, little brat," Bella said sharply. "And who are you? The new maid, I suppose. Well, you won't last long here if that's how you talk to your elders and betters."

"You were bullying her," Maisie said, trying to sound calm. She would be a lot more careful if she actually needed her job at the school. Lizbeth and Florence wouldn't have been able to answer back like this. Maisie could go home as soon as she'd solved

the mystery. She shivered. If her job truly
depended on keeping a whole schoolful
of quarrelling girls on her good side, she
wouldn't last a week.

Bella smirked at her, and tugged Lucie's
hair again – so hard that Maisie was worried
she might actually pull it out.

"Stop it!" Maisie hissed, and smacked Bella's hand away. The older girl was so shocked she actually did let go, and she stepped back, staring thunderstruck at Maisie. Then she turned round and stalked out of the schoolroom. The look on her face was poisonous.

"You slapped her!" Clarissa whispered, wide-eyed.

"You really did," Arabel agreed, in case Maisie might not have noticed.

"Thank you, Milly!" Lucie squealed, throwing her arms round Maisie's waist and hugging her tightly.

"I'd better finish mending your pinafore," Maisie murmured. And if Bella had gone crying to Miss Prenderby, she had better finish it soon. She might get the sack before teatime.

"You really smacked Bella?" Alice whispered to Maisie the next morning, as Maisie put down a rack of toast in front of her at breakfast.

"How did you know about that?" Maisie asked, frowning. She hadn't had a chance to speak to Alice the day before.

"The little ones have told everybody!" Alice pointed out. "They're still all giggly about it. And Bella is in the worst mood ever."

"I know. I'm surprised she hasn't told Miss Prenderby on me," Maisie muttered.

"She probably thinks she'll get into trouble for being mean to Lucie. But Maisie, I'm absolutely sure that she'll do her best to pay you back. Be careful, won't you?"

"Miss Fleet's watching," Maisie murmured, passing on to the next group of girls.

The young teacher was eyeing them disapprovingly. The maids weren't supposed to chatter with the pupils.

"Come to my room later!" Alice breathed, out of the corner of her mouth.

After breakfast it was Maisie's job to tidy the girls' rooms, though there were so many that some of the work would have to wait till after lunch, especially as she and Lizbeth would be called down for other things like answering the front door, and carrying morning tea. But it meant that she could go and talk to Alice quite easily, just by deciding to tidy up her friend's room first.

"You've been ages!" Alice complained, jumping at Maisie as soon as she opened the door and pulling her into the room.

"I can't talk for long, Alice," Maisie warned, starting to make Alice's bed, which was tricky with Snowflake curled up in the middle of it, and the kittens playing hide-and-seek in the sheets. "There's a lot to do."

"I know." Alice went round to the other side of the bed and tried to help. She was actually making the bed harder to straighten, but Maisie didn't want to tell her so. "Listen, Maisie, this is important. First of all, you really must watch out for Bella. She's still got a face like a thundercloud, and I'm sure she means to do something horrible to you. And second, Monsieur Allan comes this morning – the dancing master," she added, when Maisie looked confused. "I do think he's awfully suspicious, Maisie. So can you try and have a look at him? Perhaps he's the thief."

Maisie nodded. "I'll try."

Alice beamed at her. "Don't worry. I have a plan!"

Maisie was making Arabel's bed when Arabel herself dashed in. "There you are, Milly! You have to come down to the music room at once. Alice knocked over a vase of flowers while practising the polka, and there's water all over the floor."

"Oh, did she indeed?" Maisie muttered to herself. Alice's plans always seemed to spell trouble. Still, at least she would get a good look at Monsieur Allan.

Maisie could see what Alice meant about him as soon as she crept through the music room door with her mop. He was ludicrously tall and thin, and he was wearing the skinniest trousers Maisie had ever seen. She supposed this was to make dancing easier, but he looked quite ridiculous, especially as he'd added a very fancy waistcoat. And he had the strange pointy eyebrows that Alice had mentioned, as well as the world's teensiest moustache, like a slug perched on his upper lip. It was all Maisie could do not to giggle.

Monsieur Allan beamed at her and waved her at the puddle of water, before he went on drilling his class in their steps.

Maisie couldn't nose too openly, as Miss Fleet was there playing the piano, but she wasn't quite sure why Alice found him so suspicious. Yes, he was rather odd-looking, and his French accent was much thicker than Madame Lorimer's. He sounded as though there were several bees tucked into his sunken cheeks – every time he said anything he managed to put extra zs into it.

"And ze steps again! And zis time with ze happiness!"

But that didn't make him a thief.

After a few minutes of watching the class while she mopped, Maisie decided rather sadly that Alice might not like Monsieur Allan simply because she didn't shine in his dancing classes. She kept mixing up the steps, so that the dancing master had to push her and her partner back into the right place.

"Ah! Eeet eees eleven o'clock! Ze class
is feeneeshed. *Au revoir, Mesdemoiselles.*"
Monsieur Allan swept a deep, graceful
bow and mopped his damp face with an
embroidered handkerchief.

Miss Fleet hurried the girls away to
change out of their dancing slippers, and
Monsieur Allan and Maisie were left in the
studio. The dancing master was tidying
up the silk scarves and tambourines that
the girls had been using for their country
dancing. Maisie scurried around and picked
them up for him – there seemed to be scarves
trailing all over the furniture.

"Ah, *merci beaucoup*!" The Frenchman
smiled at her. "Most helpful!"

"Don't forget your handkerchief, sir,"
Maisie reminded him, picking it up off the
floor. "It would be a great pity to lose it,"

she added. "It's so pretty." The cloth square
was beautifully embroidered with a trail of
ivy leaves around the edge. It was far nicer
than anything Maisie would be able to sew.

"Ah! My wife, she sew him for me,"
Monsieur Allan explained, tucking the
handkerchief away in his pocket. "She ees
ill, you see? She lies on a sofa all the day,
and she sews." He sighed, shaking his head.
"I must be off, another class to teach." He
smiled sadly at Maisie. "Ze doctor's bills,
you see, zey are very costly. I work at many
different schools." He looked down at his feet,
rather embarrassed, as though he had said
more than he should have done.

Maisie nodded thoughtfully. Her first
proper case had involved money stolen from
the local butcher's shop, and the thief had
been a girl desperate to pay for medicine for

her poorly sister. Sally was now working at
31 Albion Street, as she had lost her job at
the butcher's when Maisie discovered her. But
Maisie didn't think that Monsieur Allan was a
thief. He wouldn't tell people about his need
for money, would he? And if he were stealing
gold bracelets, he wouldn't need to teach so
many classes.

"Sir, which days do you teach here?" she
asked suddenly.

"Tuesdays and Thursdays," he told her
smiling. "*Au revoir, Mademoiselle.*"
And he swept Maisie a courtly
bow, which made
her giggle.

Maisie held the door open for him, and went to put her mop away, frowning to herself. She had got Alice to write her a list of all the different things that had been stolen, or possibly just lost, and when their owners thought they'd disappeared. There wasn't any sort of pattern that Maisie could see, and the thefts certainly hadn't happened only on Tuesdays and Thursdays. She pulled the list out of her apron pocket and studied it. No pattern to the days at all, and none to the things that had been taken either. A gold bracelet. Dancing slippers. Kid gloves. Someone's favourite – most definitely not new – china doll.

Nothing in common. Except that people loved them... Maisie decided, as she wandered slowly along to the cupboard.

The bracelet could be sold for a lot of

money, if you found somewhere where the buyer wouldn't ask questions. But no one would pay much money for an old doll, even though Miss Lydia had been terribly upset. The only thing the stolen goods had in common was that they were valuable to their owners.

It was as if the thief just wanted to make people miserable.

Chapter Seven

Thinking about the times of the thefts had made one thing clear to Maisie – this was definitely an *inside job*. Not a delivery boy, or anyone just visiting. It had to be one of the girls, or a member of staff. Or even possibly one of the teachers, although Maisie thought that was doubtful. Miss Prenderby's livelihood depended on keeping her young charges and their parents happy – and Miss Fleet was just too plain silly to be a thief.

On balance, Maisie was leaning towards the thief being one of the pupils. The maids were too busy for playing silly tricks like stealing dolls and dancing slippers. Stealing worthless treasures was a spiteful young lady's game, she thought.

But then some of the girls, like Bella and Frederica and Marianne, were incredibly rude to the servants. She had seen Marianne screech at Lizbeth only this morning, just because the maid hadn't had time to make her bed. Maisie was sure that if she had to put up with that sort of thing, day in, day out, she'd be tempted to teach the stuck-up little misses a lesson too.

Maisie was almost sure that Lizbeth wasn't the thief, though. Maisie had seen inside the maid's attic room, and there was simply nowhere that Lizbeth could hide all those things. There weren't even any loose boards in the floor – Maisie had checked.

Maisie clicked the broom-cupboard door shut and leaned on it wearily. She felt as though she'd done a day's work already. It was hard enough getting all her jobs done, let alone trying to fit in detecting as well. And now she had to go back to tidying up the young ladies' rooms. She brightened a little. It was quite likely that one of the girls was the thief, so surely there must be a clue or two, lying around in their bedrooms. And she could go searching, and just say that she was tidying up. Maisie hurried up the stairs with a little more energy. She had been beginning to think there was no point in her being here – that Alice could have done the detecting herself. But Alice couldn't go snooping around as easily as a maid.

Now which of the young ladies should she investigate first? There were twenty-five girls at Miss Prenderby's, and almost everyone had had something stolen, or thought they had. As far as Maisie could see, there was no reason to suspect any of them more than the others.

Maisie sighed as she looked around Bella's room. She had made the bed earlier on that morning, but she hadn't had time to tidy up. Bella was one of those girls, like Alice, whose parents paid larger fees for her to have a bedroom and a little sitting room of her own – and she made the most of it. Clothes and papers and a box of expensive French chocolates were strewn around. Maisie couldn't quite work out how Bella had managed to make such a mess since she had tidied up the day before. It looked as if she had opened up her wardrobe and flung most of the contents in the air.

Maisie hurried around, picking up the garments, and trying to work out where they went. She tucked several pairs of pretty kid slippers into the bottom of the wardrobe, next to an enormous sealskin muff. Bella really did have the most ridiculously smart clothes for a schoolgirl. Her drawers were all full to bursting, with stockings and petticoats trailing out of them. Even when Maisie had taken everything out of Bella's stocking drawer and refolded it, the drawer still didn't want to close properly. Muttering crossly to herself, Maisie yanked it out again, and felt around down the back of the drawer, to see if something had fallen down behind.

"Ah… Got you!" Triumphantly she pulled out a ball of something greyish-white. A screwed-up pair of kid gloves, with pretty embroidered cuffs.

Exactly like the ones that Florence was supposed to have stolen.

Maisie sank down on to the floor, spreading out the gloves on her apron and staring at them. Had they simply fallen down the back of the drawer by accident, or had Bella hidden them on purpose, so that she could blame Florence? There was a mark across the palm, a brownish stain, like tea perhaps. Had Bella accidentally spoiled her nice new gloves, and decided to use them as a chance to pick on Florence?

Maisie darted quickly into the sitting room, opened the door, and peered out down the stairs. No one was coming. She went back to the chest of drawers, and pulled out every drawer, peering into the gaps. But there was nothing else hidden down there, and she didn't have time to search the whole room.

I'll be back, Maisie thought to herself angrily, tucking the gloves away in her

apron pocket with her list. If the rest of
the stolen things were hidden in here,
somewhere, she would find them. And she
would make sure that everyone knew what
Bella had done.

"You think Bella stole them herself?" Alice
whispered, as she unfolded the gloves later
that afternoon. "What for?"

Maisie shrugged. "To get Florence into
trouble? I don't really know. She's horrible
to everybody, as far as I can tell. I don't
know why she'd want to blame Florence
particularly."

Alice nodded slowly. "I do. Florence
spilled a dish of chops in gravy all down
Bella's dress, a few weeks back. It was
before I came, but Florence told me about it.

She said Bella was absolutely raging. I suppose this is Bella's way of getting her own back." She frowned. "But if that's why, I'm not sure that Bella can have taken the other things. I think Clarissa's gold bracelet went missing before that. A month ago, she said."

"Hmmm…" Maisie whipped round and started dusting the schoolroom mantelpiece as Miss Fleet walked past the open door. Alice pretended to be searching for something in the bookcase.

"That was close," Maisie muttered. "Do you think she heard us?"

"I don't think so. Oh, but Maisie, your wig is on a little bit crooked. Here." Alice twitched it straight, and rearranged the little frilly cap on top. "That's better."

Maisie sighed. She was growing to hate that wig. She longed for bedtime now, not just because she was so tired from running up and down stairs all day, but also because she got to take the horrible thing off. It was heavy and it itched.

That night, Maisie sank down on to her lumpy bed, and yawned sleepily. Then she slipped the fair wig off, and shook out her crushed red curls. She had just finished changing into her nightgown, and was about to climb into bed, when stealthy little footsteps padded up to her door, and someone stifled a giggle.

"Who's that?" Maisie called quietly. She didn't want to wake Lizbeth next door.

"It's only us, Milly," a squeaky little voice called back, and Maisie smiled. It sounded like Lucie.

"Shh! Come in then!" she called.

As she'd expected, it was Lucie, Clarissa

and Arabel. All three of them were giggly and
excited as they bundled through the door,
but then they came into the light of Maisie's
bedside candle, and stared.

Maisie stared back, wondering why they had gone so suddenly silent. And then she remembered. The wig! She had been so sleepy, she'd simply forgotten that she'd taken it off.

"You've got *red* hair!" Lucie whispered at last.

"Yes…" Maisie admitted.

"But why were you wearing a wig?" Arabel asked. "Is it because people called you names?" she asked sympathetically. She had reddish hair too, though not nearly so red as Maisie's, and some of the other girls called her Ginger or Carrots.

Maisie sighed. She hated to lie to them. For the sake of the case, she probably should, but they were so little, and so nice.

"No. It's because I'm in disguise," she explained. "And my name's not really Milly

– it's Maisie. I'm a friend of Alice's. She asked me to come and work here, to see if I could find out who's been stealing things. She doesn't believe it was Florence, you see."

"Oh, we don't either," Clarissa agreed. "Are you a detective? Like Gilbert Carrington?"

Maisie was about to say, *Well, sort of*, but then she remembered that she had helped to solve a case that had baffled the police a few weeks before. "Yes," she said, going a little pink. "I am." Although a real detective wouldn't have minded lying at all, she thought sadly. And now the little girls were bound to go and tell Miss Prenderby, or Mrs Elkins the housekeeper.

"Can we help?" Arabel asked hopefully. "I'd *love* to be a detective."

Maisie blinked. "You aren't going to tell Miss Prenderby who I really am then?"

"Of course not! If you find the real thief, you might get my bracelet back!" Clarissa pointed out. "I haven't told Papa I've lost it yet…"

"Do you know who it is?" Lucie asked, curling up on the end of Maisie's bed and staring at her curiously.

"Yes, do you have a *suspect*?" Arabel asked, trying out the unfamiliar word carefully.

"Well… I think so," Maisie admitted. "I found the gloves that Florence was supposed to have stolen from Bella. In Bella's own room."

"In that case, I most definitely want to help," Lucie said determinedly. "I hate Bella. If she's a thief, she'll get sent away, and that would be wonderful."

The other two nodded seriously, and

Maisie shivered. She didn't like Bella either, but she couldn't help imagining what it would be like to be hated by everyone. Even the girls like Frederica and Marianne who hung around Bella didn't really seem to like her that much.

"You'd better go back to bed," she told the little girls. "You'll get into trouble if you're caught up here."

They did as they were told, with a lot of giggling and shoving, and Maisie just hoped that they'd make it back to their own rooms without being caught.

Then she wriggled back down under her patched sheets and lay there, thinking. Lucie, Clarissa and Arabel seemed to have taken all her sleepiness with them.

Maisie had the next afternoon off – she was allowed every second Wednesday – and she was going home. She had promised Alice that she would make sure Florence was all right, and she wanted to see Gran. Maisie missed her a lot, and she missed Eddie even more.

She walked demurely round the side of Russell Square, but as soon as she was out of sight of the school, she ran! She reached home half an hour later, red in the face and panting, and practically flung herself through the kitchen door.

Eddie had been lying on a folded blanket by the stove, and he leaped up and danced around her, barking wildly, until Maisie picked him up. Then he did his best to lick her thoroughly all over.

"Oh, I missed you too!" Maisie told him, laughing. "Not my mouth, Eddie. Yes, good boy. Hello, Gran!"

"When you've quite finished letting that creature slobber all over you, Maisie, I've made scones," Gran said grimly, but she kissed Maisie's hair, and got licked by Eddie too, as he was so excited he didn't know what he was doing.

"Ugghh. Put that dog down! Come and have some tea, for heaven's sake, and let me look at you."

She gazed at her granddaughter. "Are they feeding you properly?" she asked, frowning.

"Yes. The cook's very good, even if she is as mean as anything." Maisie gulped down her tea gratefully. "How's Florence?"

"Hmmm." Gran looked thoughtful. "I never thought I'd say this, Maisie, but I wish she was

142

more of a chatterbox like you. I swear, you could mistake that child for a mouse, she's so quiet. Always talks in a whisper. Luckily the dog likes her. She's been walking him for you – not far, just up and down the street. I wouldn't trust her not to get lost otherwise."

The kitchen door opened then and Sally the maid came in, followed by Florence herself. Maisie thought she looked much better than she had at Miss Prenderby's – as though she didn't expect someone to tell her off any minute. Maisie's gran was strict, but she was very fair, and she liked people who worked hard.

Maisie beamed at her. "Hello, Florence! Alice sends her love."

Florence smiled back, but didn't say anything, just quietly slipped into her place at the table and sipped her tea.

"So have you solved this mystery yet?"
Sally asked.

Maisie sighed. "I think I might have done.
But I'm not sure. And I don't know how to
prove it either."

"Who do you think it is?" Florence
whispered.

"Bella," Maisie said, watching Florence
to see what she thought.

Florence didn't look very surprised.

"I found those gloves she said you stole, you see," Maisie explained. "They were shoved down the back of one of her drawers. I couldn't find the other things, though."

"But I thought you told me that Miss Bella was one of the richest of the girls," Gran said to Florence, with a frown. "Why on earth would she want to steal?"

"Because she's mean," Florence whispered. She had gone pink in the face, and she was almost shaking with anger. She suddenly looked a lot less like a mouse.

Maisie nodded. "All the things that were taken were special," she explained slowly. "They were the girls' favourite things, or they were important, or new. Things that people would be really upset to lose. Someone chose them carefully, to make people as miserable as they could. And Alice thinks Bella might have hidden her own gloves to get Florence into trouble," Maisie explained. "Something about spilling gravy on her?"

Florence looked ashamed. "I did. But it was an accident."

"This Bella sounds like a nasty piece of work." Gran sniffed. "Why is that, Maisie?"

"What do you mean?" Maisie asked,

looking puzzled.

"Well, she must have a reason," Gran pointed out. "She's a fortunate young lady, it sounds to me. Why should she be mean?"

Maisie nodded slowly. "Clarissa did say something that made me think. Bella's family are somewhere abroad – her father is a diplomat. So she never gets to go home, or that's what it sounded like," she added doubtfully. "She's been at the school for years."

"She never goes home?" Sally asked, sounding horrified. "That's awful. How old is she?"

"A bit older than me?" Maisie wondered. "Maybe twelve or thirteen?"

Florence nodded. "Thirteen. And she hasn't seen her parents in six years, Lizbeth told me so."

"Well, it's no excuse for stealing," Gran said doubtfully. "But I do feel sorry for her."

Maisie nodded. She seemed to have solved the mystery, but she wasn't sure it actually helped. She still needed to get Florence her job back. And Bella couldn't be left to keep on taking people's things and bullying the other girls. But Maisie didn't want to make things any worse for Bella than she had to.

Chapter Eight

"Milly – I mean, Maisie…" Lucie stopped, looking confused.

"You'd better still call me Milly," Maisie suggested. "Someone might hear you."

Lucie nodded. "Where have you been? I've been looking for you for ages."

"It was my afternoon off," Maisie explained, as she hung up her coat and hat on the hooks in the back corridor where the staff kept their outdoor things. "Is something the matter?"

"Oh no," Lucie explained happily. "I just wanted to show you. My mother came to visit, and she brought me a present, look!" She held out her wrist, and showed Maisie a beautiful silver bracelet, with little charms dangling off it.

"That's very pretty," Maisie said admiringly. "I like the little dog," she added.

"I know! I can't decide if he's my favourite, or the soldier. My father is in the army, you know." Lucie paused. "What's the matter, Milly? You've got such a frown."

"I was just thinking," Maisie murmured. "No, don't worry. I don't expect it would work."

"What? What?" Lucie squeaked. "Tell me!"

"Well, I expect you've shown your charm bracelet to everyone," Maisie said slowly. "So all the girls know that you have it, and that it's special. Someone who wanted to make trouble for you might try to take it – like all the other special things that have gone missing."

"But I won't let anyone, Milly," Lucie said earnestly. "I'll look after it, ever so carefully. I shan't let Bella anywhere near it!"

"Exactly," Maisie agreed. "It's too precious,

that's why I said my plan wouldn't work."

"Oh, Milly! Are you going to set a trap for her?" Lucie exclaimed.

"I was thinking about it." Maisie nodded. "But I don't want anything to happen to your bracelet."

Lucie nibbled her bottom lip. "I'd get it back, though, wouldn't I? And I do want to get rid of Bella, Maisie. She makes everyone miserable."

"I wasn't thinking of letting her steal the whole bracelet," Maisie explained. "But we could undo one of the charms, you see. And then if you could drop it, just when she happens to be walking by, and pretend that you haven't noticed…"

"She would pick it up!" Lucie breathed.

"Yes. And if we were watching, perhaps we could spot where she's hiding things.

I've looked everywhere I can think of in her rooms while I've been cleaning. I think she must have another hidey-hole somewhere."

"Let's do it!" Lucie agreed eagerly.

"I have to get back to the kitchens, or Mrs Albert will be looking for me," Maisie explained. "Can you go and find Alice, Lucie, and explain to her what we're going to do? Ask her to open the link on the dog charm with her penknife. Here, look." She pointed to the place. "If she leaves it just a little loose, so that you can pull it off easily, then that should work. And then you'll have to watch out for the right moment to drop the charm." Maisie thought for a moment. "I won't be there to help, but if you tell Alice and Clarissa and Arabel, then between the four of you, you must be able to see where Bella goes."

Lucie nodded. "I'll go and tell Alice now,"

she said, as she hurried back along the
passageway.

Maisie watched her go and sighed. It was
a good way of catching Bella in the act, but
she had hoped to find some way of solving
the mystery without getting the older girl into
trouble. She felt sorry for her.

"Maisie! Maisie!" Alice dashed into the music
room, where Maisie was dusting. It was the
next afternoon, and Maisie had been waiting
nervously to see whether Lucie would be able
to carry out the plan. Lucie was so little and
so giggly, Maisie wasn't sure whether she
could convince Bella.

But it seemed she had. Alice was dragging
Maisie along the corridor towards the back of
the house and the kitchens.

"Where are we going?" she asked. She had assumed that Bella would have hidden the things somewhere in the main part of the house.

"Wait and see," Alice said grimly. "There! Look!"

Lucie, Arabel and Clarissa were standing by Maisie's coat, hanging on its peg.

"What on earth are you three doing?" Maisie asked in surprise.

"We followed her!" Lucie explained. "We hid behind the broom cupboard and watched."

"And guess where she put it!" Clarissa added.

"You'll *never* guess!" Arabel folded her arms triumphantly.

Maisie looked at her coat, and thinned her lips. "She's doing it again, isn't she? She was furious with me for standing up to her when she was mean to Lucie. Has she put it in my pocket?"

The little girls looked disappointed, but then Lucie nodded. "I suppose you really are a detective. Yes, look!" She dug her hand into the pocket and pulled out the little silver dog.

"You'd better put it back," Maisie said slowly. "We can use it to show Miss Prenderby what Bella did to Florence… Wait a minute! Where's Bella now?"

The other four gaped at her.

"Didn't you look?"

They shook their heads worriedly, and Alice gasped, "Do you think she's gone to tell?"

"Yes!" Maisie yelped, looking around wildly, as though she expected Miss Prenderby to appear out of the woodwork any moment.

Alice grabbed her arm again, and they dashed upstairs, the little ones hurrying after them.

"What are we going to do, Maisie?" Alice panted. "We can't prove that you didn't take that charm. Oh, perhaps we shouldn't have left it there!"

"We'll tell Miss Prenderby it was Bella," Lucie suggested eagerly, but Maisie shook her head.

"I don't know if she would believe you. You're the littlest girls in the school, and Bella – well, she can be very convincing when she wants to be. No one's going to take my word over Bella's either, I'm just a maid."

"No, we can make sure no one thinks it was you, Maisie," Alice said firmly. "Lucie, come on, we're going to your room. You lost your charm, and you called me and Arabel and Clarissa and Maisie, I mean Milly, to help you find it."

"Good idea! Come on." Lucie scurried along the landing, and they all followed her to the room she shared with the other little ones.

"And before we came to help, Maisie, you were in my room," Alice whispered. "Helping me tidy up, because the kittens tipped out my sewing basket! Miss Prenderby will believe me, I'm sure of it."

There was a sharp knock on Lucie's door just as Alice finished, and Miss Prenderby marched into the room, followed by Bella. "What on earth are all you girls doing in here?" the headmistress snapped.

"Oh, Miss Prenderby, my little dog charm has fallen off my bracelet!" Lucie squeaked, when Alice nudged her. "I asked the others to come and help me, and Milly too. I wanted her to help me lift up the chest of drawers. I think the charm might be underneath."

Maisie stared at her admiringly. Lucie was much better at making up stories than Alice.

"I have your charm," Miss Prenderby said coldly, holding it out.

Lucie took the little silver dog, trying to look surprised. "Thank you! Where was it, Miss Prenderby?"

"It was in this girl's coat pocket." Miss Prenderby gazed at Maisie. "Where she put it. Bella has just told me that she saw Milly pick something up a few minutes ago, and then she went sneaking along so suspiciously that Bella decided to follow her."

Alice frowned. "But Milly was with me until a few minutes ago, Miss Prenderby. The kittens had knocked over my sewing basket, so I asked her to help me clear it up. All my embroidery silks were knotted up and it took us ages. Nearly an hour."

Bella stared at Alice, and her mouth dropped open. She obviously hadn't expected Maisie to have an alibi.

"Are you quite sure?" Miss Prenderby

asked sternly.

"Oh yes," Alice said. "Bella must have been mistaken."

"I wasn't…" Bella muttered, but she looked worried. It was her word against Alice's.

"Milly *was* in Alice's room – that's why Alice came to help us look for the charm too," Lucie put in. Only Maisie could see that she had her fingers crossed behind her back.

Miss Prenderby turned to look at Bella, who quailed under her searching gaze. "Well?"

Bella's mouth opened and shut, but she didn't say anything.

"All of these girls say that you're mistaken, Bella, but I really don't see how you can be. You can't have imagined seeing Milly take the charm and put it in her pocket. You either did see her, or you made it up."

"It was a mistake," Bella muttered, scarlet-faced.

Maisie frowned. Miss Prenderby certainly suspected Bella, but this wasn't quite good enough. They needed to help Florence get her job back.

"Miss Prenderby, may I visit my grandmother this afternoon?" Maisie asked suddenly, pulling Bella's stained gloves out of her apron pocket. "I found these gloves in one of the young ladies' rooms, and they're all stained. My gran has a book of recipes for cleaning, and I'm sure she'd know something I could use to get the marks off."

Maisie held out the gloves to Miss Prenderby, who turned them over in her hands, frowning. "Kid gloves... Embroidered kid gloves. Bella, aren't these the gloves that—"

"Where did you get those?" Bella shrieked at Maisie. "What were you doing looking in my stocking drawer?" Then she realized what she'd said, and clapped her hand across her mouth, looking horrified.

"You said *Florence* took your gloves!" Alice said angrily. "You made it look as though she was a thief, and she hadn't stolen anything at all! And now you're doing it again to Milly!"

Bella stared sulkily at her feet, but she said nothing. It was obvious that, for once, she couldn't think of any way to shift the blame.

"Bella, come with me!" Miss Prenderby snapped. "You will go to your room, and I shall be sending a telegram to your parents, explaining that you cannot stay here any longer!" And she stalked away, with Bella following hangdog after her.

Two weeks later, when Maisie went back to the school to visit, Florence opened the front door to her and hugged Maisie delightedly. Maisie thought she looked as though she'd settled in – she was pink-cheeked and not so thin and nervous.

Lucie and the others had been so pleased to see her that it was some time before Maisie managed to escape upstairs to talk to Alice.

"Did the little ones tell you?" Alice asked, when she finally got Maisie to herself. "Bella's been sent off to Vienna, or wherever it is her parents are, with a friend of Miss Prenderby's to be her governess. And do you know what? Bella actually asked Miss Prenderby to let me come and see her, and she gave me all the things she'd taken! She wanted me to give them back to everybody."

"Where were they?" Maisie asked curiously. It still made her cross that she hadn't been able to find them.

"In her wardrobe, tucked inside that huge sealskin muff she was so proud of."

"Oh! I looked in the wardrobe, but I never thought to look inside *that*!" Maisie clicked her tongue irritably.

"The strange thing is, Maisie, I think Bella was almost glad she'd been caught. She told me that she wrote and explained to her parents how much she wanted to be with them instead of at school the whole time, and so she's going! They'd sent her to school because they keep travelling around, and they thought she'd be lonely without anyone else her own age. And her mother has a terrible fear of her catching typhus fever in foreign cities, apparently. But Bella wrote to her that she'd rather have typhus than stay at Miss Prenderby's any longer. And I think Miss Fleet wrote too, and told them that Bella needed to be with her mother and father."

Maisie nodded. "I hope she'll be happy now.

But how's Florence?" she added worriedly. When Maisie had given in her notice, Alice had told Miss Prenderby that she'd sent Florence to work at her father's house, since she'd felt sorry for her. Maisie hadn't really wanted Florence to go back to Miss Prenderby's, to have to sleep in that horrible little room and spend all her time avoiding the grumpy cook. But Florence had said she liked it, with all the girls. It reminded her of the Foundling Hospital, she said. And it was a lot more comfortable, even with the lumpy bed.

"Florence is much happier now Bella's gone. Everyone is! I know you thought it wasn't all her fault, Maisie, but she was still nasty."

"She was," Maisie agreed. She smiled at Alice. "I do miss working here, you know. It's very quiet back at Albion Street. And it was lovely being able to see you all the time." Then she shuddered. "I don't miss that awful, itchy wig, though. It was worth it, for the sake of solving the mystery and getting Florence her job back, but it's so nice to just be me again!"

Have you read?

The Case of the Stolen Sixpence

When Maisie rescues an abandoned puppy, he quickly leads her to her first case. George, the butcher's boy, has been sacked for stealing, but Maisie's sure he's innocent. It's time for Maisie to put her detective skills to the test as she follows the trail of the missing money…

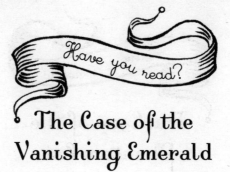

Have you read?

The Case of the Vanishing Emerald

When star-of-the-stage Sarah Massey comes to visit, Maisie senses a mystery. Sarah is distraught – her fiancé has given her a priceless emerald necklace and now it's gone missing. Maisie sets out to investigate, but nothing is what it seems in the theatrical world of make-believe…

Have you read?

The Case of the Phantom Cat

Maisie has been invited to the country as a companion for her best friend, Alice. But as soon as the girls arrive, they are warned that the manor house they're staying in is haunted. With Alice terrified by the strange goings-on, it's up to Maisie to prove there's no such thing as ghosts…

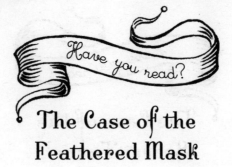

Have you read?

The Case of the Feathered Mask

Maisie loves to look at the amazing objects her friend Professor Tobin has collected on his travels around the world. But when a thief steals a rare and valuable wooden mask, leaving only a feather behind, Maisie realizes she has a new mystery on her hands…

Have you read?

The Case of the Secret Tunnel

Gran has a new lodger and Maisie suspects there's more to him than meets the eye. Fred Grange says he works for a biscuit company, but he is out at odd hours and knows nothing about biscuits! Determined to uncover the truth, Maisie is drawn into a mystery that takes her deep underground…

Find out more about Holly Webb

www.holly-webb.com